BINKY RULES

A Marc Brown ARTHUR Chapter Book

BINKY RULES

Text by Stephen Krensky

Based on a teleplay by Sandra Willard

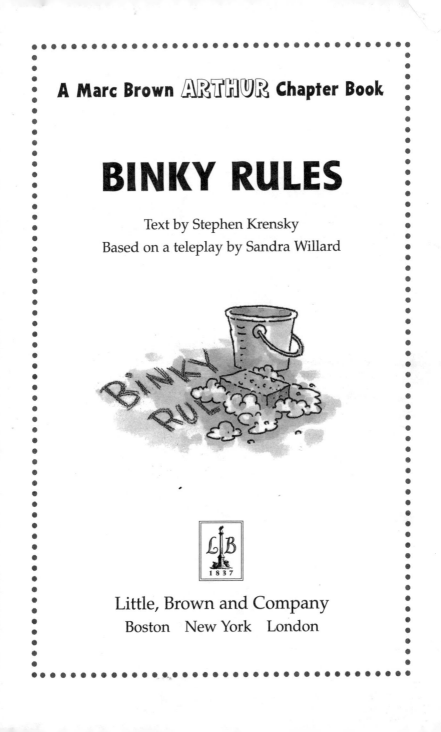

Little, Brown and Company

Boston   New York   London

ISBN 0-316-12244-0

LCCN 00-041231

10 9 8 7 6 5 4 3 2 1

WOR (hc)
COM-MO (pb)

Printed in the United States of America

For Shea Quadri, O.T.N. —
One Terrific Nephew

Chapter 1

• • • • • • • • • • •

The students at Lakewood Elementary School were making a lot of noise at recess. But Mr. Morris, the custodian, was used to that. He paid no attention to all the yelling and laughter. He had work to do. Raising his clippers, he carefully trimmed the last of the bushes near the gym.

When he finished, he stepped back to inspect his work. Mr. Morris was well known for the saying "Every school should take pride in its students and in its appearance."

His eyes swept the length of the building. The bushes were neat, the grass was green, and the —

Suddenly, Mr. Morris gasped. There, right in the middle of the walkway, two words were written in yellow chalk.

BINKY RULES

"Binky rules?" Mr. Morris looked annoyed. At his school nobody "ruled" by writing on school property. This was totally unacceptable.

Over on the playground, Francine rolled a ball toward Binky Barnes. He let the ball roll up his foot, then he tapped it up into the air repeatedly.

"Seven . . . eight . . . nine . . . I might break my own record."

Francine looked impressed. "You'll definitely make the traveling team, Binky."

"You think so?"

"Absolutely."

Binky smiled. He let the ball drop to the ground — and then gave it a big kick.

The ball sailed way over Francine's head.

Across the playground, Arthur, Sue Ellen, Buster, and Muffy sat around Muffy's portable radio. They were listening to a new song.

"This is the best song *ever!*" said Muffy.

Arthur nodded. "It makes you want to dance. I wish the station would play it all day long."

"Maybe then we could find out what it's called," said Buster. "Oh, oh, here comes the end. Pay attention, everyone."

"That's our most requested song today," said the DJ. *"Now for the chatter on the platter. It's the surprisingly popular —"*

Binky's soccer ball flew in, knocking the radio over. It was suddenly quiet.

"Oh, no!" Everyone groaned.

Francine and Binky ran over to join them.

"Was that a kick or was that a kick?" said Francine.

"It was a kick, all right," said Binky.

"I'm glad you settled that," said Muffy. She grabbed the radio and turned it back on. But it was too late. The DJ was gone. All they heard was a commercial.

Arthur sighed. "Now we'll have to wait even longer."

"I heard the group is Finnish," said Buster. "Maybe we could call the United Nations."

"Buster," said Arthur, "I think the United Nations has better —"

"BINKY, COME HERE!"

Everyone turned around. It was Mr. Morris yelling.

"What did you do?" Buster asked Binky. "When Mr. Morris yells like that, it's a bad sign."

"When anybody yells like that, it's a bad sign," Sue Ellen pointed out.

"He's wearing his 'You're in big trouble' face," said Arthur. "What did you do?"

Binky shrugged. "Nothing. At least, nothing I remember."

"Well," said Arthur, "I think you're about to get your memory jogged."

Chapter 2

• • • • • • • • • • •

Mr. Morris waited for Binky to walk over to him. His arms were folded, and his foot tapped against the ground.

"You called me?" said Binky.

"Yes, I did." Mr. Morris stopped his tapping.

There was a long pause.

"Is anything wrong?" Binky asked.

The custodian eyed him closely. "We have to have a little talk. You've been going to Lakewood a long time, haven't you?"

Binky nodded.

"I thought so. And do you find the rules of the school confusing?"

Binky nodded again.

"Ah. Well, what about the idea of not damaging school property? That seems clear enough, doesn't it?"

"I guess," Binky admitted.

"Good. Then how do you explain this?"

He pointed to the walkway, where BINKY RULES was written.

"Wow!" said Binky. "Cool!"

Mr. Morris shook his head. "No, Mr. Barnes, it's not cool. Not cool at all. This is a mark against the walkway, a scar on the face of the school."

"Oh."

Mr. Morris knelt down for a closer look. "You may think that because water will wash this chalk away, it doesn't really count as graffiti."

"Graffiti?" said Binky. He looked confused.

"Yes, graffiti — the scribbling of words or pictures across walls or buildings. It is an ugly practice, Mr. Barnes."

"I've never seen my name that big before," said Binky. "It looks really, um, large."

"And you never should see it that way again. This is wrong, Mr. Barnes, and you should know better. This is graffiti as sure as if you had carved it in stone."

Binky scratched his head. "Wait a minute! You think I did this?"

"Can you think of anyone else who would have a reason to write your name?"

Binky had to admit he couldn't. "But I didn't do any graffiti-ing," he insisted. "I haven't been over here all day."

"Mr. Barnes, do you think these words just grew here?"

Binky frowned. "That's a hard question. Science isn't my best subject."

"Well, take my word for it," said Mr. Morris, "it's not possible."

"Okay."

"So, that leaves me with only one conclusion and one culprit: you. And since you went to so much trouble to create your name here, it is only fitting that you spend the proper time removing it. I've got the hose and brush right here. You can spend the rest of recess cleaning it up."

"But what about soccer . . . and kickball . . . and tag? . . ."

"Mr. Barnes . . ."

Binky sighed. When Mr. Morris used that tone, there was no point arguing. Picking up the hose in one hand and the brush in the other, Binky got to work.

Chapter 3

. . . .

"Binky rules?" said Arthur.

"That's right," said Binky.

They were standing outside Mr. Ratburn's classroom at the end of the school day. Buster and Francine were there, too.

"But you didn't write it?" said Francine.

"Nope."

"Was it hard to clean up?" asked Buster.

Binky nodded. "Mr. Morris didn't want even the smallest smudge left behind. He said it would be a blot on the school's honor."

"Do you think someone was playing a trick on you?" asked Buster.

Binky shrugged.

"Well, then," said Arthur, "is anybody especially mad at you?"

Binky stopped to think. "No more than usual."

The four of them started down the hall for the side exit.

"It is too bad, though," Binky went on. "If I had brought my camera, I could have taken a picture. I might never have another chance to see my name that big again."

He pushed open the double doors and walked outside. The others followed.

"I mean, something like that happens once in a lifetime."

"Uh, Binky . . . ," said Buster.

"I could be old and gray without ever seeing —" said Binky.

"Well . . . ,"Arthur began.

"— a sight like that again."

"BINKY!" Francine shouted. "Look!"

She pointed back the way they had come. There, on the double doors they had just passed through, two words were written so big that each covered half a door.

"BINKY RULES," said Buster, reading from one door to the other. "Wow! You've been busy."

"But it wasn't me," said Binky. "Honest. I mean, it looks great, but I didn't —"

"Well, no matter who did it," said Arthur, "if Mr. Morris sees it, you'll be camping out in the principal's office for the rest of the year. We need to clean this up — and fast."

Moving quickly, the four of them went to the supply closet for water, sponges, and a bucket. They managed to get back to the doors without being questioned and began washing off the chalk letters as fast as they could.

"Thanks for helping, guys," said Binky.

"I never had to wash my name off a door before. It is kind of exciting."

"Never mind that," said Arthur. "You have a problem here. A weird problem. Why would someone write your name all over the school?"

"It's mysterious," said Buster. He nodded knowingly.

"Mysterious, as in *mystery*," said Francine. "Come on, Binky. We need someone to solve this problem."

Buster stepped forward, clearing his throat.

"And I know just who to ask," said Francine. "Fern."

She dragged Binky away.

"Why didn't she ask you, Buster?" asked Arthur. "After all, you're a detective. You solved the mystery of the missing quarters."

Buster didn't know. He dipped a sponge in the water and kept scrubbing.

16

Arthur picked up a sponge to join him. "You could solve this. I know you could."

Buster scrubbed some more.

Arthur looked around. "But we have an even bigger mystery here," he said.

Buster looked up. "What's that?"

"How come we're the only ones still scrubbing?"

Chapter 4

• • • • • • • • • • •

"Where are we going?" asked Binky.

Francine grunted. "To see someone whose razor-sharp mind will get to the bottom of your problem."

"Who's that?"

Francine walked over to Fern, who was reading under a tree.

"Hi, Fern!" said Francine. "We need your help."

"You do?"

"Well, not me exactly," said Francine. She explained about Binky and what had happened earlier in the day.

"Hmmm," said Fern. "So this mysterious graffiti has already shown up twice?"

"And it wasn't my fault either time," Binky insisted.

"Do you have an alibi?" asked Fern.

"A *what?*"

"An *alibi.* Proof that you were somewhere else at the time the crime was committed."

Binky frowned. "Well, we don't know when that time was."

"So you have no alibi." Fern frowned.

"I can't help that," Binky insisted. "I didn't know I was going to need one."

"Of course you didn't," said Fern. "Besides, a person who wrote graffiti using his own name wouldn't be very smart."

"Hey, that's right!" said Binky. "I hadn't thought of that."

Fern and Francine exchanged a glance. "Uh-oh!" they said together.

"Really!" said Binky. "I'm innocent." He looked at Arthur, who was walking up with Buster. "Tell them, Arthur!"

"Tell them what?" Arthur asked.

"That I'm telling the truth."

Arthur shrugged. "I can't say for sure. A judgment like that should come from a trained professional. Someone like Buster, for example. He's a *real* detective."

"But not the only one," said Francine. "Fern found my bracelet, remember?"

Arthur did not look impressed. "Buster found money. That's what real detectives find."

"Is that so?" said Muffy, who had arrived with the Brain just in time to hear the end of this. "Girls actually make the best detectives. Did you ever notice that there are two Hardy Boys but only one Nancy Drew?"

Arthur frowned. "So what?"

"Well, I think it's obvious. It takes two of them to do the same detecting as one of her."

"You're oversimplifying the situation," said the Brain. "The Hardy Boys solve complex problems. Nancy Drew gets criminals to confess by charming them with her smile."

"That's not true!" Muffy declared.

"The Hardy Boys," said the Brain, "confront dangerous situations, while Nancy Drew doesn't even get her fingernails dirty."

"Oh, pleeeeeeease!" said Francine. "Don't make excuses for the Hardy Boys. They couldn't detect their way out of a paper bag."

"Oh, yeah?" the boys shouted.

"Yeah!" the girls shouted back.

"WAIT!" said Binky.

Everyone turned to him.

"As the one the mystery concerns the most, I'd like it if we all worked together. Then I get the best of all of you."

Everyone was surprised to hear Binky say this, because it made so much sense.

"All right," said Buster.

"I guess so," said Fern.

"Good," said Binky. "Now, go do your detecting — and please, make it fast."

Chapter 5

• • • • • • • • • • • •

The next morning Buster and Fern met before class to plan their strategy.

"We have to act fast," said Fern.

Buster nodded. "Pretty soon the trail will be colder than a penguin's tootsies."

Fern gave him a look. "Anyway, this may be a case where we want to work both forward and backward," she said.

Buster frowned. "What does that mean?"

Fern opened a notebook and consulted the first page. "We go forward by examining the graffiti site. We look for clues that may lead us to whoever's responsible. But we can also work backward from the idea that whoever is doing this is trying to get Binky in trouble. Otherwise, there's no point in using his name. So if we can figure out who that is, we may be able to catch them in the act."

Buster stared at her. Fern sounded just like a character out of a book. "You thought that up all by yourself?" he asked.

She nodded. "I've read a lot of mysteries, and it's very important to get yourself to think the right way."

"I guess thinking is important," said Buster, "but you have to act like a detective, too. People tend to spill the beans when they believe you've got them cornered like a rat on a sinking ship."

"I suppose . . . ," said Fern. "I never thought about it quite like that. Either way, I think we should interview some witnesses. We should start with Mr. Morris."

That made sense to Buster. After all, Mr.

Morris had been the first to find BINKY RULES. "Okay," he said agreeably.

Then he saw the Brain and Arthur signaling to him, making faces and waving their hands. At first he didn't understand what they were doing, but then he figured it out.

"Wait a minute, Fern!" said Buster. "Who put you in charge?"

"Well, nobody," Fern admitted. "Do you have a different idea?"

Then she saw Francine and Muffy signaling to her, making faces and clenching their fists. At first she didn't understand what they were doing, but then she figured it out.

"Actually, it doesn't matter if you do," said Fern. "I'm the more experienced investigator."

"Oh, really?" said Buster. "Says who? I already found the first piece of evidence — yellow chalk used by the perp."

"The perp?"

"The perpetrator," Buster explained. "The one who wrote the graffiti." He rolled his eyes. *It's always tough dealing with amateurs,* he thought.

"Let's see it," said Fern. "Maybe there's a brand name or fingerprints or . . ."

Buster started to pull the chalk from his pocket, but all he came out with was a handful of yellow dust.

Fern laughed. "First rule of detecting, Buster: Never sit on your evidence."

Chapter 6

• • • • • • • • • • •

Fern was in the custodian's office talking to Mr. Morris. Buster was supposed to meet her there, but he had not shown up on time. So she had started without him.

"You say you left that sidewalk unattended while you went to get Binky?"

Mr. Morris stopped to think. The radio was playing in the background, but Fern ignored it.

"It was only for a minute," he said finally. "I didn't see anyone else around."

Fern wrote something in her notebook. "And has this sort of thing ever happened before?" she asked.

"Not where a student was mentioned by name. It was —"

A shadow suddenly fell between them. Fern and Mr. Morris both turned to see Buster standing in the doorway. He was wearing a trench coat and a floppy hat.

"Thanks for doing the warm-up, sister," he said to Fern. "I'll take over the Q and A."

Suddenly, the unknown pop song started playing on the radio.

"That song!" gasped Buster.

Mr. Morris looked over to the radio. Then his glance fell on the clock next to it. "Hey, it's after three. I've got to get back to work."

He ushered Buster and Fern out of his office and locked the door. "I'll see you kids later."

Buster didn't seem to be paying attention. He knelt down and pressed his ear to the door, trying to hear the song.

"Phooey," he said, straightening up. "It's not on loud enough."

Fern glared at him. "Who cares about that silly song? Do you see what you did? You distracted our witness! You ruined the whole interrogation."

Buster pushed back his hat. "Don't blow a fuse, doll face. What's next?"

"What's next? I'll tell you what's next! Stop talking that way and get rid of those dumb clothes."

"Everybody's a critic," said Buster. "Now if you're done jabbering, let's take a look under the hood."

They moved to the walkway where the graffiti first appeared. Fern knelt down on her hands and knees, studying the cement and making notes in a notepad. She spotted a footprint in the dirt, but before she could get a better look, Buster had stepped into it.

"Do you see what you did?" Fern yelled.

Buster took another lick of his lollipop. "Listen, pinky crooker, this evidence stuff is all smoke and mirrors."

Fern frowned. "Am I supposed to understand what you're saying?"

"Very interesting!" said Buster. He reached into his pocket and pulled out a candy wrapper. He scribbled on it.

"Can we move on?" asked Fern.

At the formerly graffitied door, Fern took a close look as Buster leaned against the wall.

Fern threw up her hands. "I can't find anything we can use."

Buster nodded. "I know what you mean. Looks like Binky's taking the pancake fall."

"Will you please speak English?!"

Buster removed his hat. "Nobody seems to know anything, Fern," he said seriously. "I think that's very odd."

"You're the one who's odd, Buster. I think maybe Binky did write the graffiti, and he's making me work with you so that I won't learn the truth."

She stormed off, leaving Buster writing on his candy wrapper again.

Chapter 7

• • • • • • • • • • •

Fern was sitting under a tree making sketches of the key players in the mystery. Sometimes she found that drawing had a way of helping her collect her thoughts. She had drawn Binky, Mr. Morris, even herself. And now she was working on Buster. Everyone else in her sketches looked perfectly normal, even better than normal. Buster, however, had his eyes crossed and his tongue sticking out.

Suddenly a scoop of ice cream landed on the sketch.

Fern looked up. Buster was standing

there. He had sneaked up behind the tree to see what she was doing.

"Oops!" he said.

"Were you spying on me?" asked Fern.

Buster shook his head. "Me? Hardly. It is true, of course, that a detective should be able to see without being seen, but I wasn't practicing. I was just passing by." He glanced at the sketches. "I have to say, though, it doesn't look like you're making much progress."

"Progress!" cried Binky, coming up behind them. "That's the word I wanted to hear. In fact, the more progress, the better. I'm glad to see that you two are working so well together."

"That's us!" said Buster.

"We're quite the team," Fern said dully.

"Great!" said Binky. "So tell me — what have you found out?"

Buster cleared his throat. "After considering the whole situation in great detail

. . . and assembling the different clues and interviews . . ."

"Yes?" said Binky.

". . . Fern has decided that you did it yourself."

"What?" Binky turned to Fern.

"That's not true!" she insisted.

"It's what you said," Buster reminded her.

Fern looked embarrassed. "Well, um, you didn't understand what I meant. You see, Binky, it's so obvious that it's you, that it's obviously not you."

Binky folded his arms. "Say that again?"

She did.

Binky scratched his head. "I didn't understand that any better the second time." He sighed. "But I do understand that you have no other suspects."

"We haven't given up yet," said Fern.

"True," said Buster. "Don't worry. We'll

unravel the whole enchilada before the cat gets out of the bag."

Binky just nodded, because it didn't seem to help when he asked anyone to repeat things. "Well, I hope you get some results soon. I'm so nervous about this, I can't even kick a ball right."

He drop-kicked his soccer ball and watched it bounce off some trees before rolling away down a hill.

"Hey! Come back here!" he shouted, chasing after it.

"Poor Binky," said Fern.

Buster swallowed. "If we don't find some solutions soon, he could be up the creek in the pokey for sure."

They stared at their notes.

"I have one *possible* idea . . . ," Fern began.

"Um, so do I," said Buster.

"Okay, what's yours?"

"You first."

"No, you first."

Buster snorted. "I bet you don't even have an idea."

"I do, too!" Fern insisted.

"Then what is it?"

"Well, what's yours?"

"You first!"

Fern groaned. "How about if you tell Mr. Morris? Maybe he'll know what to do next. Unless you think it's a bad idea."

"I'll tell Mr. Morris my idea if you tell him yours."

"Deal!"

They shook hands on it — and went off to find Mr. Morris.

Chapter 8

• • • • • • • • • • •

Mr. Morris was standing in his office when he saw the kids approaching.

"Back again?" he asked.

"Yes," said Fern, who, along with Buster, was leading the way. Binky, Francine, and Arthur walked behind them.

"Still trying to get Binky off the hook?"

Fern nodded. "We had a couple of ideas to —" she began.

"I'll take over now, Fern," said Buster. "To be honest, Mr. Morris, digging out the truth was tough. But that's the way the truth is sometimes. It was dangerous, too. But don't worry. I've figured things out."

Everyone turned to him.

Buster cleared his throat. "Hold on to your hat, because what I've discovered is that Binky . . . has an evil twin!"

"AN EVIL TWIN?" everyone else said together.

Buster nodded. "Shocking, isn't it? And devilishly clever, too." He turned to Binky. "Your twin is out to ruin your life so that he can take over your identity."

Binky gasped.

"You are kidding, right?" said Fern.

Buster shook his head. "Evil twins are nothing to kid about, Fern. You should know that."

"Oh, really?" she said. "And why would anyone, especially an evil twin, want to take over a ruined identity?"

Buster admitted that he didn't know. "Who can say how an evil twin's mind works?"

"I know I can't," said Arthur. "I have

enough trouble figuring out how D.W.'s mind works."

"Wow!" said Binky. "An evil twin. I wonder where he lives."

Mr. Morris scratched his head. "Well, Buster, I'll say one thing for you. You have an active mind."

"Overactive, I'd say," said Fern. "Mr. Morris, my theory is a bit more reasonable. The way I see it, this is the work of a rival school."

Mr. Morris frowned. "Why would another school do that?"

"Other kids know that Binky is a really good soccer player. But if he got in big trouble, maybe he wouldn't be allowed to try out for the traveling soccer team."

"That's possible, I suppose," said Mr. Morris.

"In order to expose them," Fern went on, "we'll have to catch them in the act.

We'll need motion-activated video record-ers, infrared sensors, ultra—"

"Hold on a minute," said Mr. Morris. "We don't have any equipment like that."

Fern looked disappointed. "Can't you order some?"

Mr. Morris looked pained. "That would mean a lot of paperwork. And, boy, do I hate paperwork."

"Then what can we do?" Francine asked.

"I'll keep my eyes open," said Mr. Morris. "Don't you worry, we won't let any troublemakers get onto school grounds."

The kids left the office. Francine and Fern went one way, and Buster, Binky, and Arthur went the other.

Francine snickered to Fern. "An evil twin? Can you believe Buster came up with that? You sure showed him."

"I guess," said Fern. But she didn't sound very sure of herself.

Meanwhile, Arthur was whispering to Buster. "A rival soccer team? What an imagination! Where does she get this stuff? You sure showed her."

"I guess," said Buster.

But he didn't look like he meant it, either.

Chapter 9

· · · · · · · · · · ·

As school was letting out the next day, Fern ran into Buster outside the main office. They had avoided talking during the morning and early afternoon, but Fern decided enough was enough.

"Look, Buster," she began. "About yesterday . . . um, I want to —"

"Me, too," said Buster. "I mean, I don't think I'm a better —"

"Good day, everyone!" said Mr. Morris, coming up behind them. "The sun is shining, and all is well. No sign of trouble, I trust? No soccer players on the loose?"

Fern shook her head.

"No evil twins skulking about?"

Buster shook his head, too.

"Excellent. Then perhaps the crime wave has passed. Maybe we can —"

He stopped talking as he caught sight of the school wall outside the window. BINKY RULES was written there in big block letters.

"Again?" they all said together.

They went out for a closer look.

"It's hard to tell about the handwriting," said Fern. "But have you noticed the letters are always in yellow?"

"Yellow chalk," Buster added. He knelt down at the bottom of the wall. "And look, here's a little piece broken off." He stopped to think. "You know, it takes a lot of chalk to make that many big letters. I wonder where they get it."

"What about the hardware store?" said Mr. Morris.

Fern nodded. "And if they bought

enough of it at once, Mr. Geary might remember."

Buster nodded. "Then what are we
waiting for?"

When they arrived at the hardware store,
Fern and Buster found the owner, Mr.
Geary, inspecting a new shipment of
paintbrushes.

"Hi, Mr. Geary," said Buster. "We have a
question about chalk."

Mr. Geary smiled. "Only one?"

"At least at the moment. We have a
piece of chalk that we were wondering
about. Do you sell chalk here?"

"And did anybody buy a lot of it?"
added Fern.

"Ah, you see," said Mr. Geary, "we're
up to two questions already. Let me have
a look."

He took the chalk from Buster.
"Hmmmm . . . this might have broken off

from the Number Five Lemon Custard. Then again, it could be the Daisy Sunshine. Sometimes the yellows are hard to tell apart."

Buster sighed. "Can't you check under an electron microscope or something?"

"Nope. But even if I could, I don't sell either one, so I won't be of much help. Now, if you want to know something about paintbrushes, let me know."

They said good-bye to Mr. Geary and walked outside.

Fern sighed. "That was our best chance. We've failed Binky."

As they unlocked their bikes, Buster stopped. He heard music.

"Hey," he said, "it's that song again."

Fern groaned. "How can you think of music at a time like this?"

But Buster wasn't listening. He wheeled his bike around and followed the music.

As he rounded the corner, he suddenly stopped. And stared.

Fern pulled up behind him. She stared, too.

They couldn't believe their eyes.

Chapter 10

• • • • • • • • • • • •

"Scrub harder!"

Mr. Morris had already said this several times to Binky, who was doing his best to erase the latest version of BINKY RULES.

"Come on," Mr. Morris went on, "put some muscle into it."

Binky pressed harder. *If I do have an evil twin, why does he have to write so big?* he wondered.

Mr. Morris might have said more, but he was distracted by the sound of music coming from the street. He and Binky turned their heads as a yellow van with the red letters WELM on the side stopped at the curb. Fern and Buster suddenly popped their heads up through the sunroof.

"It's not an evil twin," announced Buster.

"Or a rival soccer team," shouted Fern.

They pointed to a banner over the van. The banner proclaimed "BINKY RULES!"

All of the commotion drew Arthur, Francine, and the others from the playground.

Fern and Buster came out of the van with the radio DJ.

"BINKY is the name of that group," said Buster. "You know, the one we kept hearing."

"This is my fault, guys," the DJ explained. "I told my staff to go around town and stir up interest in the band. I guess they went overboard."

As the interns scrambled out of the van, the DJ pointed them toward the remaining chalk letters.

"Start cleaning! And after you finish that, we'll think of a few more things for you to fix up."

As the staff rolled up their sleeves, the DJ rolled up his own and dug into a cardboard box. "To make up for all the trouble, free CDs for everyone!"

Fern and Buster exchanged a grin. Then they shook hands.

"Good work, detective," said Buster.

"You, too, detective," said Fern.

Arthur turned to see how Binky was reacting and was surprised to find him looking a little disappointed.

"Binky, what's wrong? You've been cleared. You should be happy."

"I know."

"So what's the problem?" asked Francine.

"This means there's no evil twin," said Binky. He sighed. "I miss him already."

Whatever Arthur or Francine said next

was drowned out as the DJ blasted BINKY's new song over the van speakers. Buster put on his detective hat and started to dance with Fern.

"Hit it up, Twinkletoes! I'm in Nada-ville!"

"We both are," said Fern. "Whatever that means."

Then she laughed.